My Christmas Treasury

Brown Watson

ENGLAND

Printed in the German Democratic Republic

Contents

The Night
Before Christmas

It's the night before Christmas, but, for Tom and Jane, it hardly seems like Christmas at all. They have just moved into a new home, so there has been no time to put up any decorations or to find a place for a Christmas tree. Hardly any Christmas cards have arrived, and, as if that were not enough, their Daddy is away on business.

Mummy has gone next door to see if she can borrow something to decorate her Christmas cake. But, Tom and Jane are still not very happy.

"There's nowhere to hang our stockings," says Tom sadly.

"No chimney for Father Christmas, either!" says Jane, almost in tears.

"Wait a minute," says Tom, almost in a whisper. "Wasn't that a tap at the door?" "Mummy coming back, probably!" answers Jane. But, when they go to see who it is – guess who steps into the room! That's right - it's Father Christmas, carrying a sack!

"Don't look so surprised!" he tells Tom and Jane. "I know most people expect me to come down chimneys, but that's usually very uncomfortable, you know. I find it's often rather inconvenient, too – don't you?" Tom and Jane do not know what to say. But they are very pleased to have such a jolly Christmas visitor.

"I know I'm really supposed to wait until you are asleep," adds Father Christmas, "but I thought you would like a surprise. The best Christmas presents are always nice surprises, aren't they?" And he puts a pretty basket of snowflake candies on the table, together with a box of the loveliest Christmas crackers Tom and Jane have ever seen!

Then, with one last cry of "Merry Christmas!" he is gone. They look out of the window, but there is no sign of the man with the white beard and red suit. Could it really have been Father Christmas, come to see them? "Look, Tom!" cries Jane suddenly, pointing to somebody walking up the path, carrying a lantern. "Carol singers!"

When Tom and Jane go to answer the door this time, it isn't carol singers at all! No, its Mummy – and Daddy, who has managed to arrive home in time for Christmas!
"Merry Christmas, Tom and Jane!" he says, smiling behind a pile of Christmas packages and parcels. "Sorry, I couldn't come down the chimney!"

Tom and Jane wonder if Daddy pretended to be Father Christmas – until they see their Christmas stockings on the window sill! "Merry Christmas!" comes the cry as a sleigh flies across the starry skies. And now, with Daddy home, Tom and Jane know what Father Christmas meant about the best presents being the nicest surprises.

Jingle Bells

Dashing through the snow,
In a one horse open sleigh,
O'er the fields we go,
Laughing all the way.
Bells on bob-tail ring,
Making spirits bright,
What fun it is to ride and sing
A sleighing song tonight!

Jingle bells! Jingle bells!
Jingle all the way!
Oh, what fun it is to ride
In a one horse open sleigh!

Jingle bells! Jingle bells!
Jingle all the way!
Hoorah for good old Santa Claus!
Hoorah for Christmas Day!

The Story of Christmas

Christmas is the time when we remember the story of how Mary and Joseph made the long journey to the little town of Bethlehem, where the Baby Jesus was born in a stable. They had to put their names on a list of everyone who had to pay taxes.

Tom and Jane and all their friends have been working very hard. They have been getting ready for their Nativity Play. This will tell the story of that first Christmas. There is so much to do! Everyone has had to learn their part and try on their costumes.

Mums and Dads have been busy too. They have sorted out lots of things like towels and old shirts to make the right sort of clothes for everyone in the play. And one Daddy has even brought a rocking horse to school! This will play the part of the donkey, which Mary rode for most of the way, with Joseph leading it along.

At the time of the first Christmas, lots of people had to make the same journey as Mary and Joseph. So, when they reached Bethlehem, all the inns were full. Mary was so tired, because her baby was about to be born.

"I do have a stable," said one kind inn-keeper at last. "It is not much, but at least it is dry and warm."

The Baby Jesus was born in that stable. There was no cradle so Mary laid Him in a manger – very like the wooden box which Tom and Jane use in their play. The first people to see Jesus were some shepherds, with the bright, shining star guiding them to the place where He lay.

14

Three wise men had followed the star, too. When it stopped over the stable, they knew that this was the place where the Christ Child had been born. Each one had brought something for the Baby, gifts of gold, frankincense and myrrh. The shepherds could only give Him a lamb, but Mary and Joseph treasured this just as much.

How peacefully the Baby sleeps among the hay and the straw of the stable, with the stars shining brightly overhead! Not a sound is heard as the Nativity Play tells the story of the first Christmas. All is very quiet, very still, just as it must have been when Mary and Joseph watched over the Holy Baby.

Just as these poor shepherds and the three wise men brought their gifts to Jesus, so families and friends still give presents to each other. It is a way of sharing in all the good things of Christmas, of showing that we care and want to make people happy — just like Joseph, Mary and the Baby Jesus.

Everyone claps at the end of the Nativity Play.
Then there is a lovely party with lots of nice
things to eat and drink. And when Tom and
Jane open their presents on Christmas Day,
they will be remembering the birthday of
the Baby whose story they and their
friends have told.

Santa's Sleigh

Have you ever wondered
Where Santa leaves his sleigh,
When he brings toys for girls and boys
To find on Christmas Day?

For reindeers, all the roof-tops
Are much too smooth and steep!
One slip, and they'd go sliding down,
And land in one big heap!

But if they were in the garden,
How could Santa, with his sack,
Climb right up to the roof-top,
Then down the chimney stack?

There's too much danger in the road...
So, where CAN he leave his sleigh?
Perhaps you'd like to ask him,
When he comes round your way!

The Christmas Party

Tom and Jane are on their way to a Christmas party. They are taking a big basket of mince pies which Mummy has made, and a box of Christmas crackers.
"This party is going to be extra special," Mummy tells them.
"Why is that, Mummy?" asks Jane.
Mummy gives a big smile.

"Because you will be going to many different lands!" she says. Tom and Jane cannot think what she means by that. When they get to the hall where the party is being held, Father Christmas is there, waiting with a smile and some Christmas treats for Tom and Jane. But, who are the people with him?

Tom thinks they must be friends of Father Christmas.
"Hello, children!" smiles a man with a floppy, black beret on his head. "My name is Black Peter and I come from Holland!"
"And I am La Buffana, from Italy!" says a lady in a fur-trimmed dress. "Don't you think I look like a lady Father Christmas?"

Before Tom or Jane can answer, in comes a dear little white goat!
"My friends from Norway brought him along to the party," explains Father Christmas. "He is the Christmas goat, Tom and Jane. He comes to bring us all some more good things for Christmas!"

"Just as long as you've been good," laughs Black Peter.
"Of course we have!" smile two other children. They know Black Peter because their daddy is Dutch. "Didn't we leave you a treat inside our clogs on Christmas Eve?"
"Clogs?" says Tom. "We hang up stockings for our presents!"

"What about a lump of coal?" smiles La Buffana. "That's what naughty children in Italy get. Try a piece!"

"It looks like coal . . . ." says Tom.

"But it feels crumbly!" says Jane.

"It's a blackcurrant sweet!" laugh two more children. "La Buffana always likes playing jokes when she brings our presents."

"Our mummy is from France," says a little girl.
"So we have brought some bon-bons!"
"Bon-bons?" says Jane, looking at the pretty
packages of lace and sugared almonds. "That's
what we sometimes call Christmas crackers!"
"Let's pull one and see what's inside!" cries
Tom. Soon everyone is having fun, sharing
Christmas treats from different countries.

Poor Old Santa!

We've put up the decorations
With plenty of holly to see,
We've helped Mummy to make
Mince pies and a cake,
We've remembered the star for our tree!

We've hung up our Christmas stockings…
But the chimney we did not clean!
Now, there's soot, dirt and mess,
Santa's stuck there unless…
He can wait 'til the chimney sweep's been!

A White Christmas

Everyone likes to see snow at Christmas time! Tom and Jane have used flour and water to paint snow patterns on the windows at home – just like the ones they have seen in the shops. And now, Jane has just finished dabbing the holly wreath on the front door with egg white and icing sugar to make it look more like Christmas!

"I wish there was some real snow!" sighs Tom, looking up at the wintry sky. "Then we could have a proper white Christmas, like the pictures we see on Christmas cards." Jane has to agree. "And it would be nice to make a Christmas snowman, Tom," she says.

"You don't always need snow to make a snowman," laughs Mummy. She takes Tom and Jane indoors and brings them a big bag of cotton wool. Soon, they are both hard at work.

"It looks just like snow, Tom!" says Jane. rolling the cotton wool into big balls to make the snowman's round body.

"But it doesn't feel cold and wet like snow!" says Tom. All the same he makes lots of snowballs. First, he wraps little presents and sweets in paper, dabs on some glue, then covers each one with cotton wool, to make snowball surprises for everyone on Christmas morning. "We'll have a lovely snowball fight!" he smiles.

"With all this talk of snow," says Daddy, "I think I had better get the sledge out of the garden shed and check it over. Then you'll both be ready for a white Christmas!"
But there is still no sign of snow. Not even one, single, tiny snow-flake. Tom and Jane cannot help feeling disappointed.

"Cheer up, you two!" says Mummy. "You won't worry too much about not having any snow when we go to see the Christmas Show." ...she takes Tom and Jane to the theatre to ...the tickets. Outside, they see all the ...ces and posters about the show, and they ...very excited. Can you guess which one ...are going to see?

Yes, it is Snow White and the Seven Dwarfs! Tom and Jane enjoy every minute. But the most exciting part comes when one of the dwarfs says:

"Is there a boy and a girl here who have been wishing for a white Christmas?"

"Yes!" Tom and Jane shout out. "We have!"

The dwarf comes to take Tom and Jane by the hand, and leads them up on to the stage. Then they help to teach all the people a song about Father Christmas bringing every̶ And̶ snow at Christmas. The wonderf̶ buy̶ with a shower of fairy snow-flake̶ notic̶ gently down. "So we got our wh̶ are v̶ after all, Jane!" laughs Tom. they̶